THE BLADE OF FIRE

Other Gladiator Boy titles to collect:

GLADIATOR BOY

THE BLADE OF FIRE

DAVID GRIMSTONE

*Hodder
Children's
Books*

A division of Hachette Children's Books

First published in Great Britain in 2009
by Hodder Children's Books

2

A Catalogue record for this book is available from
the British Library

ISBN: 978 0 340 98911 1

Typeset by Tony Fleetwood

Printed in the UK by CPI Bookmarque, Croydon, CR0 4TD

The paper and board used in this paperback by Hodder Children's Books are
natural recyclable products made from wood grown in
sustainable forests. The manufacturing processes conform to the
environmental regulations of the country of origin.

Hodder Children's Books
a division of Hachette Children's Books
338 Euston Road, London NW1 3BH
An Hachette UK company

www.hachette.co.uk

For Doris Christina Minter (er ... then Stone, then Ford) my many-named grandmother.

I would like to dedicate the entire Gladiator Boy *series to* Terry Pratchett. *There is no writer, living or dead, for whom I have greater respect. Thank you for everything.*

CONTENTS

ANCIENT ITALY

PREVIOUSLY IN GLADIATOR BOY

Forced into a deadly quest by overlord Slavious Doom, Decimus Rex finds himself in the twisting labyrinth beneath the legendary Arena Primus. Determined to rescue an unconscious Gladius, he and Olu are frozen to the spot with terror as a roar erupts around the cavern and the rescue attempt becomes fraught with new danger . . .

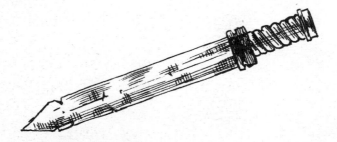

CHAPTER
I

A LONG
WAY
DOWN

Another ear-splitting roar rumbled through the meadow, but Decimus and Olu bravely soldiered on.

'If that thing is still a long way away,' said Decimus, nervously peering around him, 'it must be absolutely enormous.'

Olu nodded. 'We better keep moving, then.'

The attempt to rescue Gladius started off badly, as Olu tripped over the big slave in an initial effort to take hold of him. This caused Decimus to lift more weight than he was prepared for, and the two friends suddenly found themselves flat on the grass beside their floored companion.

Olu reacted quickly, and sprang to his feet almost immediately, snatching great handfuls of Gladius's tattered tunic. For his part,

Decimus took hold of his friend's legs and lifted with all his might: compared to the chained cage, Gladius turned out to be surprisingly light.

The two slaves crossed the cavern floor in just a few seconds, and didn't stop there, allowing their momentum to carry them through the archway and into the cavern beyond. So desperate were they to leave the enchanted meadow, however, they almost made a critical mistake.

Realizing they wouldn't be able to stop themselves in time, Decimus suddenly cried out. Once again, Olu's reactions were swift, and he half lowered, half dropped Gladius on to the rocky ledge. The move was swift, but not quite swift enough for Decimus, who released his own grip on the slave's legs a moment too late and pitched forward on to the bridge.

Olu gasped, and tried desperately to reach out for his friend . . . but Decimus was way beyond his grasp. The young slave crashed through three of the rotted bridge planks but managed to take hold of the lower support rope in order to save himself from a deadly fall.

Instinctively, Olu looked up at the cavern roof, where the vast colony of bats were hanging. He could just about make them out, the only light being a dim glow spilling from the torch still wedged in the grass of the enchanted meadow.

Nobody moved.

Decimus hung from the bridge, too frightened to haul himself back for fear of making a din. He had tight hold of the rope, which felt remarkably sturdy considering the state of the bridge.

Olu, meanwhile, stepped over Gladius and

crept to the end of the ledge, dropping on to his stomach and sliding a short way on to the bridge. Hooking his foot around one of the supports, he stretched out both hands and beckoned to his friend.

'Decimus!' The call was barely a whisper, but it seemed to echo around the chamber like a scream. 'The ropes aren't safe! Take hold of my hands! I've got my foot hooked on the support! I'll pull you up!'

'Shh!' Decimus replied, keeping one hand firmly on the rope and reaching out with the other until his fingers closed around Olu's wrist. 'OK!' he whispered, repeating the move with his remaining hand. 'Go!'

Olu prepared himself for the weight of Decimus, but his foot slipped from the support at the last second, and he found himself dragged towards the edge of the chasm at high speed.

'Arghgh!'

The cry echoed around the walls, and all at once the bats exploded into life. Every one a winged menace, they quickly turned the chasm into a sudden, terrible hive of activity.

Decimus was too surprised by the events to make any sort of grab for the rope he'd been clinging to. Instead, he tightly shut his eyes and said a prayer to the gods as he and Olu slid towards their inevitable doom.

Determined that his friend should not share in his fate, Decimus tried to wriggle free of Olu's grasp, but the other slave wouldn't let him go.

'What are you doing, you idiot!' he cried, twisting and turning in the air. 'Let go, Olu! Save yourself! Now!'

Olu slid further forward; now, his upper body was only a gnat's wing from the edge of the drop. Bats flapped madly all around them.

'If you go down with me, I swear I'll kill you!' Decimus screamed, realizing the stupidity of the threat even as it left his trembling lips.

'You wouldn't let me go!' Olu cried, trying to shout over the cacophony of the bats.

'Yes I would! YESSSSS. IIIII. WOULLLLD!'

'Liar!'

Olu cursed the gods as his strength ran out. He suddenly shot forward, and he and Decimus screamed as they both plunged into the chasm.

The bats flew all around them, and it was only when the wings of one slapped Decimus directly in the face that he realized he and Olu were still alive. What's more, they hadn't fallen.

'Olu?' he said, waiting for the skinny slave

to drop his terrified expression and open his eyes. 'What happened?'

Olu started at the question, but didn't move a muscle.

'I don't know,' he mumbled. 'It must – I must have – I don't know.'

Decimus was about to reply when they both shifted upward in a series of short, sharp bursts.

'What the—'

'Hold on! Something's got hold of my ankles! It's got claws! Arghghgh!'

Olu disappeared over the edge of the bridge, and Decimus found himself dragged along with him. At length, he clambered over the edge of the boards and collapsed, puffing and panting, on the ledge. Olu was lying beside him, eyes wide with surprise, as the bats flew back to settle on the roof of the cavern.

'You boys do get yourselves into problems, don't you?' said Gladius, letting go of the skinny slave's ankles and rubbing the dust from his hands. He smiled, widely. 'Oh, and I don't have claws, Olu – it's your skin – it's like paper.'

Olu muttered under his breath, as Decimus found himself shaking with laughter.

CHAPTER
II

CHOICES

'Thanks for getting me out of that room, by the way,' Gladius said, as the three slaves picked their path, slowly and carefully, along the rope bridge. They had adopted a method of crossing the perilous drop that involved only one of them proceeding at a time. 'I might have ended up lying there for ever if you hadn't rescued me.'

'What happened?' Olu asked, keeping still as Decimus moved around him in order to advance: he'd retrieved the torch from the meadow and was now leading the group onward. 'Did you eat one of those flowers?'

'Ha! No, it was just a bad coincidence, I think. When I found the room, I was tired anyway – Argon and I had just swum

through that flooded tunnel. We managed to
avoid the cages in that horrible room next
door . . .'

'Lucky you,' said Olu, resentfully.

'. . . and then we arrived here. I felt tired, so
I picked a patch of flowers and just sat down
for a bit. By the time I realized what was
happening, I was too weak to stand up. I
suppose Argon would have tried to move me,
but he must have given up and gone on alone.'

'Quiet!'

Decimus had reached the edge of the bridge
and was peering into the passage beyond,
holding out a hand behind him in a gesture
that warned the others to stay back.

'What is it?' Olu whispered

'Yeah,' said Gladius craning to see. 'I don't

fancy hanging around on this bridge if we can move on with—'

'Shh!'

Decimus took several steps forward and waved the torch around for a few seconds. Then he motioned for the others to join him.

The corridor beyond was long, low and filled with traps, seemingly all of which had been sprung by the poor unfortunates who wandered in before them: Decimus hoped his missing friends hadn't come this way, but all the evidence suggested they had.

Spears jutted from the walls, circular blades protruded from the ceiling and a dozen shattered crossbow bolts littered the floor.

'I know what you're thinking,' said

Gladius, as his companions both gawped at the scene. 'But if Argon or Ruma did go through here, surely they'd still be  impaled – I mean – stuck here in some state of – well, you know what I'm saying . . .'

'Unfortunately, yes,' said Olu, glaring at him. 'And I'm all for not walking on this floor at all. Maybe we can go back and try our luck with the crocodile . . .'

'These traps weren't set off by floor plates,' said Decimus, confidently. 'They were set off by wires stretched across the corridor.'

Gladius frowned. 'How do you know that?'

'Because I can see the last one at the end of the passage, and it's still active . . . so we need to be REALLY careful, here.'

Without another word, he began to move cautiously through the corridor.

'Wait!'

'Decimus, are you crazy?'

Ignoring the hushed calls from his friends, the young slave picked his way along the corridor, moving around the first set of spears in a zigzag trail and then crouching to creep beneath the two circular saws that stuck out from the roof of the tunnel. He didn't take any chances crunching through the pile of crossbow bolts, however, choosing instead to leap them completely.

He then took an
exaggerated step
over the practically
invisible wire and
pointed down at it
from the other side.

'Come on, you
two!' he called,
urgently. 'It's safe if you walk where I did.
Whatever you do, DO NOT trip on this line:
those holes in the wall look like arrow slits!'

Gladius and Olu both hurried through the
corridor, careful not to move too far outside
the areas Decimus had walked in.

When they had both safely crossed the
trip-wire, Decimus raised the flaming green
torch once again. The light revealed a

T-junction in the rough stone tunnel, giving them a choice of two paths.

'Left or right?' Olu ventured, peering both ways but seeing nothing but deep shadows in either direction.

Decimus shrugged, and turned to Gladius, who was at last beginning to look less tired. Evidently, saving two people from certain death and negotiating a corridor full of sprung traps really woke you up.

'You came in first, right?' he said. 'You and Argon?'

The big slave nodded.

'Doom didn't tell us why we were being sent down here, but we all guessed it was something to do with you. We waited a while for Ruma and Olu to be lowered down, but it didn't happen . . . so, after a few hours, we went wandering through the tunnels. That turned out to be a big mistake . . . for me, at least.'

Decimus nodded. 'This whole place is old . . . and I mean old. It's also full of weird things that shouldn't exist . . .'

'Like a meadow packed with flowers that put you to sleep . . .'

'Yes, and a torch that just keeps on burning even when you throw it around . . .'

'There's something up ahead that Doom is frightened of,' said Decimus, slowly. 'I don't know what it is, but I know how much he wants the thing he's sent me to get. I'm guessing whatever made that noise is the real reason Doom will not venture down here.'

'What is it?' Olu ventured. 'The thing you've been sent down here to get, I mean?'

Decimus shrugged at the question. 'A sword,' he said, distractedly. 'An ancient blade of legend that is supposed to burn with unearthly flame.'

'You don't sound that impressed by it!' Gladius laughed.

'Well, this torch glows with an unearthly flame, but it's still a torch. C'mon, let's move. This way looks as good as any.'

The three companions headed left along the new tunnel, which was much larger and mercifully empty of any traps. However, they soon stopped dead when another deafening roar shook the entire passage. This time, there could be no doubt whether or not the tremors were imaginary: Gladius managed to hold his ground, but Olu actually staggered slightly and held on to the wall in order to right himself.

Then, just as swiftly, the roar died away.

'We're NOT going down there,' Gladius warned, pointing along the tunnel and flashing Olu a look that dared him to argue.

'You're right,' said Decimus, turning back and retracing his steps along the passage. 'It is coming from that direction.'

He reached his two companions and together the group returned to the T-junction.

'What about Ruma and Argon?' Gladius whispered. 'Do you think—'

'I hope not,' finished Decimus, arriving at the junction and continuing along the right-hand path. 'If that thing has them, whatever it is, I don't think we'd stand much chance of— look out!'

There was a loud crash, and Decimus suddenly flew backwards, colliding with Olu and Gladius, who both fell against the passage walls in an effort to save themselves. The torch flew off down the corridor, illuminating a scene in the passage ahead that almost made them wish the flames had gone out. Decimus was unconscious, lying beneath a circular dish which was actually bigger than he was. A line of blood trickled from his forehead.

Standing in the corridor before them was the biggest man Olu and Gladius had ever seen. Muscles and veins stood out on its

arms, which were covered with ugly, weeping wounds. Its body was covered in thick furs, and demonic claws sprouted from the end of its cruel hands.

The face, however, set the creature apart from the human race. It had no visible mouth, two small circles where a nose would have been and a single, giant, unblinking eye that took up three-quarters of the surface of its face.

Gladius and Olu stood frozen to the spot with fear, but the creature didn't hesitate for a second. It simply charged straight into them, its frenzied claws ripping through the air all around it.

CHAPTER III

WAR!

Olu kicked himself away from the wall and managed to turn a complete somersault in the air, flipping over the head of the giant and landing awkwardly behind it.

Gladius wasn't so lucky. He took longer than his skinny friend to shake himself out of his reverie, and the great creature tore into him like a rogue spear. The pair tumbled to the ground, Gladius frantically grabbing the giant's wrists as it tried to sink its terrible claws into his face.

'Argghhh! Help meeeeee!'

Olu dropped to his knees and tried to shake Decimus awake, but the young slave was out cold.

'Help! Heelllllppp!'

Barely managing to lift the heavy plate from his friend's chest, Olu staggered the few feet between Decimus and the crazed beast. Unable to raise the plate over his head, he simply dropped it on to the creature's back. Shaking with rage or pain (Olu couldn't tell which), the Cyclops fell on to its side, but its claws were now fastened firmly around Gladius's throat. But, Gladius was fighting back. He used the momentum Olu had bought him to roll on top of the monster, grasping at the clawed hands that still constricted his throat.

A weapon, Olu thought, his mind racing. I need to find a weapon of some sort. NOW.

His searching gaze settled on the torch, still burning brightly at the far end of the tunnel, and he raced to retrieve it.

Decimus began to stir, coughing sharply when he opened his mouth. He winced and, one hand moving straight to the cut on his forehead, he attempted to roll himself over and push himself on to his feet.

Gladius was weakening. The terrible eye bore down on him, a single ball of pure hatred, as the monster tightened its grip on his neck. Realizing he had no strength left, Gladius felt himself drifting into a swoon, and his eyes began to close.

Olu hesitated for only a second, halfway between the end of the passage and the junction, the torch held in one shaking hand. Before he knew what was happening, however, Decimus had snatched his blazing burden and crossed the passage in three quick strides, arriving beside the giant and driving the torch into its midsection. The furs that covered the creature's torso caught light, and it shook violently, releasing Gladius and rounding on its attacker like a demented lion.

Decimus didn't take a step back. Instead, he ducked the giant's grasping arms and swung up with the torch, glancing a ball of flame off its chin and knocking it back.

Still half-choked, Gladius nevertheless spotted an opportunity to down the monster and quickly crouched in a ball behind its legs.

Decimus drove the torch forward again. As Gladius had predicted, the creature backed away in order to avoid the flames, tumbling over the big slave in the process and crashing on to the cold stone floor. As Gladius rolled aside, the Cyclops scrambled around on the floor of the passage, flames now burning furiously on its furs. Its thrashing fists found the iron plate, and the resulting noise filled the corridor. It was quickly answered by the now familiar roar that erupted once again, deep within the cavern. The entire passage rocked and rumbled.

'Run!' Decimus cried, turning back and
sprinting down the corridor towards Olu,
who was still in something of a daze. Gladius
chased after them, and the three companions

dashed frantically along a tunnel that seemed to go on for ever.

Finally rounding a bend in the passage, Olu saw a heavy-looking door and made straight for it. The roar had died away, but the dull thunder of the Cyclops hitting the iron plate still echoed throughout the maze.

'In here! It's open!'

Olu dashed through the door, but couldn't even move it an inch until Gladius helped by throwing his own weight behind it. Decimus pushed along with them, and the great wooden barrier was sealed.

'Get something to wedge against it!' Gladius barked. 'Quickly!'

Decimus and Olu both searched the new room they found themselves in, and soon returned to the door supporting the weight of a heavy iron plate not entirely unlike the one that had been thrown at them in the corridor.

'Wedge it under! Come on!'

Gladius and Decimus drove the plate under a beam on the lower half of the door. It wasn't exactly a fort, they all agreed, but it would have to do for now.

'You think he'll get in here?' Olu asked, nervously.

Decimus shook his head. 'No, I think he'll burn to death right where we left him, but we're not going out there until the noise has stopped.'

'What is this place?' said Gladius. He was still shouldering the door, but his eyes were drifting over the group's new surroundings.

Olu and Decimus turned to look at the chamber they now occupied. In some places, it looked like an ancient kitchen, in others it more closely resembled a museum. Stacks and stacks of bronze plates were piled in one corner of the room, while statues of different shades lined up against the opposite wall. All of them were carved in the shape of various

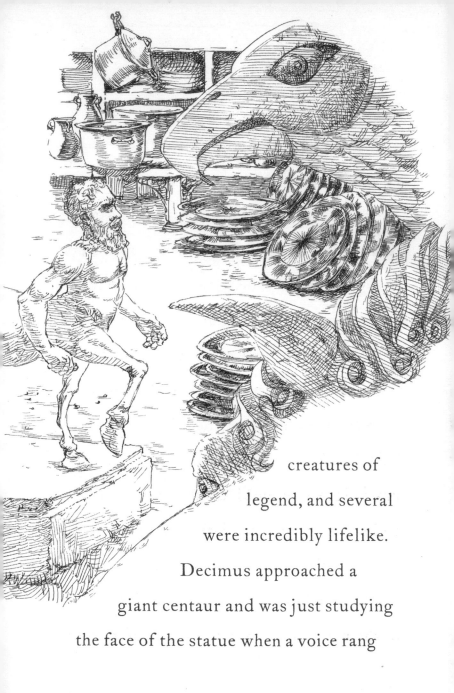

creatures of
legend, and several
were incredibly lifelike.
Decimus approached a
giant centaur and was just studying
the face of the statue when a voice rang

out and almost caused him to drop the torch he was carrying.

'Don't touch them. I think they're cursed or something.'

Olu and Gladius both spotted the speaker before their startled friend, who looked up very gingerly as if he suspected another nasty surprise at any moment.

Suspended from the ceiling on a series of tightened ropes, Ruma glared down at them.

'You took your time,' he said.

CHAPTER
IV

THE
PRISONER

'Ruma!'

Gladius started to move away from the door in order to help the chained slave, but quickly remembered why he was standing there in the first place and hurried back.

Decimus and Olu were both searching the room for a mechanism that would lower their friend, who was suspended by both his wrists and his feet.

'You have to hurry,' he spat. 'They're going to kill Argon.'

'WHAT?' All three slaves spoke together, their voices expressing the mixture of shock and terror that they felt inside. Decimus

recovered first, and quickly
continued his hunt for the chain
mechanism. Olu, meanwhile,
stopped searching and
moved to a point in the
room where he could
see Ruma's face.

'Where IS Argon?'
he said.

'On his way to the Maw,' Ruma explained,
his voice low but clear. 'They all get taken to
the Maw. It's this . . . thing that eats people.'

'EATS them?' Gladius repeated, from the
doorway. 'The other slaves, you mean?'

Ruma nodded. 'All of the ones who didn't
make the trials get brought down here. They
never see the inside of a prison cell – it's all

Doom and his lies. He feeds them to the Maw to stop it rising up and destroying half the continent . . . and, from what I've heard, it probably could.'

'How do you know all this?' Olu asked.

'Because the boy who was in here with Argon and me had been down here longer than any of the others. Once, he got into the prophecy chamber, a room somewhere in the maze with images and legends scratched into the walls. I think he also learned to understand the Cyclopeans when they spoke to each other . . . at a basic level, at least.'

'Cyclopeans?' Gladius said, nervously.

'Yeah – they're like big ogres with a single eye. It sounded like you ran into one in the corridor.'

'There are MORE of them?'

Decimus finally located the chain

mechanism behind one of the plate stacks and

unhooked several of the links, sending

Ruma crashing to the floor.

Typically, the Etrurian didn't take

very long to recover. In fact, he

jumped up and immediately

set to work with Olu,

unravelling the chains from his

wrists and ankles.

'There are three of them,'

he continued, as Decimus joined in the effort to release him. 'They're deaf, dumb and completely evil. They collect the slaves Doom throws down here, keeping them chained in this room until feeding time . . . and then they take them through to the Maw. That's why we need to hurry – they took Argon down about an hour ago.'

'But it doesn't make any sense,' Decimus argued. 'Doom sent those slaves down here to search for the Blade of Fire, surely? I know he's desperate to get his hands on it – I could see that in his eyes.'

'The boy who was taken off before Argon said the sword is supposed to be the only thing that can kill the Maw,' Ruma explained. 'Which is really unfortunate, because the

Maw guards it. Maybe Doom wants the sword because he knows no one will ever get out of the Maw's chamber with it unless they've killed the cursed thing . . .'

Ruma shook off the last of his bonds and hurried over to the far wall, where he started pushing plate stacks on to the floor.

'What are you doing?' Olu asked, as Decimus ran over to help Gladius brace the door.

'Help me move this table! They keep all their weapons in the wall behind it! Quickly! Before they get back here!'

Olu took the other end of the table, and together they managed to heave it away from the wall. Once the space was clear, Ruma ran his finger along the wall line and, finding a

small space near the bottom, pulled at the
entire section until it yawned outwards on
tired, squeaky hinges.

'In here! Look!'

Ruma reached into the crevice and passed
out a series of weapons to Olu. There was a
sword, a spear, a short throwing-axe and a
heavy-looking net.

'I'll take the sword,' Decimus said, eyeing
the blade keenly as Olu received it. 'Unless

anyone else really wants it.'

'I don't care what I get,' Gladius admitted. 'As long as I'm armed with something against those nightmares.'

'Give me the spear,' Olu muttered. 'I'm probably not strong enough to handle any of the others properly.'

Ruma kept the throwing-axe for himself and handed Gladius the net.

'We need to go over the junction to the end of the west passage,' he said. 'That's where they took all the others.'

'I guessed as much,' said Decimus, wearily. 'We were heading in that direction when we heard the cursed thing roar.'

'Everyone ready?' said Ruma, nodding at Gladius who hoisted the net on to his shoulder. It weighed a ton.

'As ready as we'll ever be,' Olu admitted.

Decimus retrieved his torch, and together he and Ruma pulled the plate away from the stout door, eventually heaving it open.

'Right. Let's go.'

CHAPTER V

THE LAIR

The slaves hurried along the western passage, Decimus leading with Ruma and Olu close behind. Gladius brought up the rear, trying to balance the net in such a way that would enable him to cast it at a moment's notice.

Decimus quickened his pace, rounding several bends in the corridor before the passage finally terminated in a high, expansive archway. He waited for the others to catch up before, muttering words of encouragement to each other, they entered the cavern beyond.

The first thing that Decimus observed about the lair of the Maw was how incredibly vast it was – a cavern so wide and so deep that it looked very much like an underground arena. It was also lit, at various points around the walls, by the same green light that had spilled from his own torch. This time, however, the light came from an entire host of torches that were clustered together in many places. A series of caves opened on to the path the slaves were standing on, all feeding into a high ledge that circled the top of the cavern.

The second thing he noticed was the Maw itself. The monster was so big that he almost mistook it for the floor of the cavern before Ruma pointed out the tentacles: these stretched right to the very roof and, in several cases, snaked into caves that led off through the catacombs. It was only when his horrified gaze followed the tentacles down to

the base of the cavern that he saw what they were attached to. The thing set into the floor looked like an enormous black ball that had become trapped inside a hole that was too small for it. An impossibly long slit ran along the middle of the surface, and Decimus guessed immediately that it would open to reveal an enormous array of teeth. The many, many eyes, which were all wide open and staring upward, covered an area so big that Decimus suspected it would take him an age simply to run across part of it. The Maw, it turned out, was practically the entire cavern.

It was Olu who first spotted Argon. The slave was hanging from a single rope that dangled him precariously over the mouth of the Maw, a rope which eventually wound

around a
hook on the
floor of the
cavern. The hook was
being guarded by the
remaining Cyclopeans,
who were also
regularly glancing at
an ornately carved
archway that simply had
to be the resting place of
the fabled sword.

'Why isn't it eating him?' Gladius
whispered, voicing a thought that both
Decimus and Olu had been wondering about.

'It's asleep,' Ruma ventured, his gaze fixed
on the mass of eyes. 'The eyes are all open,

but they're not moving.'

Decimus nodded. 'We need to get Argon down now . . . It means taking those Cyclopeans out of the problem. Gladius, Ruma – can you handle that?'

Gladius gasped at the suggestion.

'Why us?' he moaned, muttering something else under his breath.

Decimus rolled his eyes. 'Because Ruma can fight anyone and you have a massive net. Even if you don't end up beating those things, the pair of you can certainly distract them long enough to unwind the rope holding Argon. Oh, and remember – you need to do the whole thing in complete silence.'

Ruma nodded, and pinched Gladius's arm

before he could argue any further.

'What should I be doing?' Olu asked, his spear balanced carefully on one shoulder.

Decimus turned to him with a nervous smile.

'You have the most dangerous job,' he said, pointing past the group. 'You need to get on to that.'

The indicated ledge was actually a jut of rock that projected into the middle of the cavern. It was positioned not far above Argon's dangling frame.

'If that thing wakes up before Ruma and Gladius manage to free Argon, I need you to throw your spear directly into that giant patch of eyes. Do you understand?'

Olu nodded.

'How is that more dangerous than what we're doing?' Gladius muttered.

It was Ruma who answered him. 'Because the ledge is within reach of those tentacles,' he said.

'What about you?' Olu added, almost as an afterthought. 'Where are you going?'

Decimus grinned at the other slaves, and his eyes filled with a sudden, determined purpose.

'I'm going to get the Blade of Fire,' he growled. 'And then I'm going to kill the Maw.'

CHAPTER VI

THE BLADE OF FIRE

Trekking down the circular path to the cavern floor turned out to be a mammoth task all on its own. Decimus led the slave trio, his gaze shifting constantly to the Maw, to Argon and to the two giants guarding the rope hooks.

When he finally reached the floor of the cavern, it took all his willpower not to look directly at the Maw, which he correctly imagined would seem even more immense when viewed from the side.

'I'll give you a short distraction,' he whispered to his companions, raising the torch to illuminate his face, 'and then it's up to you.'

He took in a deep breath, and ran forward, drawing his sword at the last moment.

The two Cyclopeans were evidently not that alert, and Decimus had to practically walk into them before they started to react to his presence. Still, once they had spotted him, the two giants moved fast enough.

Decimus turned on his heels and ran towards the carved archway at the back of the cave. Despite the fact that he'd always been among the fastest during the trial-races, Decimus quickly discovered that he had to double his efforts in order to keep a lead on the monstrous pair. However, he didn't have to maintain that lead for very long.

Ruma erupted out of the shadows at the side of the path, crossed the cavern floor in three long strides and hurled his weapon. The axe spun through the air, blade over shaft, making a whooshing, whirring noise as it went. The throw couldn't have been better targeted; the axe head sank into the back of the first Cyclops, causing it to stagger forward and grasp at its back. Unable to scream for lack of a mouth, the creature quickly dropped on to its knees and began to flail around wildly, but Ruma was upon it in seconds.

Gladius wasn't quite as successful with his own attack. Even though he managed to cast his net fully over the second Cyclopean, he still had to charge into the creature before it went down. Within seconds, the entire cavern floor was in silent uproar.

Far above them, Olu employed a series of
careful leaps to further his journey along the
high ledge, and eventually managed to
position himself directly over
the unforgettable surface
of the Maw. He
raised his spear
in preparation to
strike, but the eyes remained
focused and unmoving.

At the back of the cavern, Decimus hurried
through the carved arch and found himself in
a small antechamber, barely bigger than the
cell he'd occupied for so many nights. The
room was lit by the now familiar emerald
fire, burning on torches all around the walls,
and the light lent an eerie glow to the

platform in the middle of the floor. It was a simple object, halfway between a table and a font, and indeed the sword itself looked – at first glance – to be nothing out of the ordinary. It didn't even glow.

Decimus approached the legendary weapon with extreme care, and reached out a shaking hand in order to retrieve it. However, before his fingers closed around the handle of the blade, something made him stop. It was almost as if he were frightened to take hold of it.

Out on the cavern floor, the battle to free Argon was intensifying. Ruma had caused his opponent no small amount of pain, first by throwing the axe into its back and then by raking his fingers across the creature's only

eye. He was currently using his well-earned

advantage to move away from the agonized

Cyclopean. Gladius was still wrestling with

his enemy: the monster had used its

incredible claws to rip its way out of the net,

but Gladius had responded by wrapping

several of the lines around its throat. Now,

he was attempting to choke it into

unconsciousness: it wasn't easy.

Still blinded, the Cyclopean attacked by Ruma had nevertheless managed to get on to its feet once again, and was pursuing the gangly Etrurian across the floor of the cavern. Unfortunately, its feet caught on the edge of Gladius's net and it came crashing to the ground, leaving the big slave with not one but two angry opponents to face.

Ruma, meanwhile, had reached the rope hooks and was suffering problems of his own. Having released the rope, he found himself dragged forward by Argon's weight. The slave, who had evidently been unconscious, quickly woke up at the sudden judder, but was alert enough not to scream in response to the shock.

'Psssst!' Ruma called, his feet scraping along the ground as Argon grew closer and closer to the face of the Maw. 'Psssst! Psssst!'

Gladius spun around, but he was now firmly in the clutches of his enemy, who had outwrestled him and currently had him locked in a reverse chokehold. Gladius twice tried driving an elbow into the Cyclopean's eye, but the monster dodged each blow. When a third thrust failed, he resorted to an old trick his father had taught him. Reaching back for the creature's head and grasping it firmly in his hands, he dropped straight on to his backside. The top of his skull crunched into the Cyclopean's chin and it staggered backwards, colliding with its companion who, still blinded, mistook it for one of the slaves and started fighting back.

Gladius rolled over the rest of the net and dashed over to Ruma. Reaching past the gangly Etrurian, he snatched hold of the rope and together they managed to hoist Argon upwards.

'Shouldn't we lower him down?' Gladius whispered, urgently.

'Into the mouth of that thing? No! Get him on to the ledge where Olu is crouching – it's his only chance to escape.'

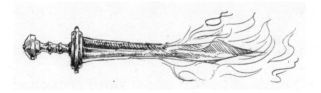

In the tiny antechamber at the back of the Maw's lair, Decimus finally plucked up the courage he had been trying to muster, and closed one hand over the hilt of the sword. He lifted the weapon very gingerly, noting as he did so that it felt as a light as a feather. As he raised the sword aloft, it suddenly ignited, and a wild blue flame licked up and down the blade.

Decimus let out a gasp of shock. It was a tiny, almost inaudible intake of breath – but it was answered by an ear-splitting roar.

CHAPTER VII

ATTACK!

O lu had never considered himself to be among the strongest of the slaves. Even so, when the unblinking eyes of the Maw suddenly flicked to the left and its indescribable jaws yawned open, he threw the spear with every ounce of strength he had in him. As Ruma and Gladius heaved on the rope that lifted Argon away from a terrible fate, the spear arched through the air and landed, with unfailing accuracy, in the middle of the vast monster's eye bank. The roar immediately changed to a scream, a powerful screech of anger that made Olu scream himself, covering his ears with both hands. Then the tentacles exploded into life, thrashing the cavern walls and tearing out great sections of rock that thundered to the ground and shattered into dust.

One tentacle struck the ledge with incredible force, blasting the ground from beneath Olu's feet. The little slave leapt into the air, threw out his arms and plummeted downward, catching on to one of Argon's legs at the last moment. The two slaves swung back and forth over the void that was the Maw's mouth.

'Don't look down!' Argon cried, his own eyes fixed upon the roof of the cavern. 'It's like staring into a bottomless pit filled with teeth!'

Olu didn't need to be told twice. He shut his eyes tightly and prayed to the gods for help.

'Pull them up!' Ruma screamed, spitting out a mouthful of dust as he and Gladius continued to haul at the rope. 'We have to get them clear of—'

He didn't finish the sentence: one of the Maw's tentacles slammed into the Etrurian and sent him hurtling across the cavern floor. A second tentacle found the struggling

Cyclopeans and dragged them, kicking and flailing, into the terrible mouth. A fountain of blood sprayed up as they were digested.

Gladius gritted his teeth, and held on to the rope, but without Ruma his feet were beginning to lose their hold on the dusty ground.

'Help me!' he screamed. 'Somebody help m—'

'Aaaaaaaaaaaaaaaarghhhhhhhhhh!'

Decimus Rex came hurtling into the cavern with a scream that almost matched the twisted roar of the Maw. He left the ground running and leapt on to the face of the

monster. Landing amid the eyes, he skimmed over a lake of mucus and blood created from the wound dealt by Olu's spear. As he slipped and slid across the glaring sockets, he drove the Blade of Fire into the surface behind him, leaving an incredible opening in his wake. Slit almost from end to end, the creature emitted a crying, screeching roar of rage that filled the entire cavern, and opened its jaws so wide that Decimus found the ground disappearing beneath him. Now, there was only the long death plunge into the creature's fathomless gullet.

In that instant, Decimus thought of his parents, and all the friends he had made in the trials. He also thought of Teo, hanging lifeless from the noose in the courtyard of Suvius Tower. So much pain, so much suffering . . . and all of it for this.

Decimus closed his eyes, released the Blade of Fire and plunged to his death . . . and the Maw yawned wide to receive its meal.

Decimus screamed out his last breath . . . and Olu's legs hooked under his arms, snapping around his chest like a vice. The slave suddenly found himself hoisted over the moving chasm, his eyes turned upward at Olu and, beyond him, Argon suspended from the rope.

'Narrghghghghgh!' Gladius screamed as he pitched, rolled and scraped forward, clinging desperately to the end of the rope.

Now, there were three bodies to support on the end of the line, and Gladius's strength was almost spent.

If he couldn't hold on another few seconds, they would all be plunged into oblivion. If he couldn't hold on ... if he couldn't hold ... if he ...

The rope slipped further from his grasp.

Then Ruma's gnarly hands locked around his stomach.

'Pull, you idiot!' screamed the Etrurian. 'You useless tub of stinking chicken grease! You mound of cow dung! Pulllll!'

Gladius bellowed like a lunatic and heaved on the rope, his legs working furiously as he dragged himself – and Ruma – backwards. The rope cranked up at high speed, piloting Decimus, Olu and Argon towards the roof of the cavern.

Far beneath them, however, something else was happening. At the moment of his suspected death, Decimus had dropped the Blade of Fire . . . and the great Maw had gulped it down.

Now, there was some sort of chain reaction

starting. A deep rumble, almost a distant explosion, had birthed deep inside the monster . . . and it was growing louder with every passing second. The beast's many tentacles suddenly tensed, as if in preparation for an impending danger.

'Just a few more feet, you festering heap of muck!' Ruma cried, the air knocked out of him as Gladius powered back a few more steps.

The suspended slaves were swiftly carried above the remaining portion of the ledge, and Decimus dropped deftly on to it. Finding his feet, he reached up for Olu, collapsing again when the slave landed directly on top of him. It was at this point that Gladius and Ruma, finally out of energy, let go of the rope. Decimus and Olu had to snatch Argon as he went tumbling past, barely managing to haul the slave on to the ledge before they set to work freeing him from the ropes that were tied around his wrists.

This done, the three friends raced along the rocky outcrop and leapt on to the neighbouring path. Then they started to dash for the bottom of the cavern, pausing in a moment of confusion when they saw Ruma and Gladius running up the path towards them.

'Get to the caves!' Decimus screamed, his eyes fixing on the motionless face of the Maw as the rumbling, rising thunder within it grew steadily louder and louder. 'It's going to explode! Get out! Get OOOOUUUTTTT!'

The five slaves didn't get all the way back to the top of the cavern. Instead, they chose an exit halfway up the path and, with Decimus urging them on via a series of frantic commands, they plunged into the dark heart of the catacombs.

BOOM.

'Run!'

BOOOM.

'Ruuuuun!'

BOOOOOOOOOOM.

The explosion rocked the very foundations of the land, destroying not only the Maw itself, the catacombs around it and the cavern above, but the whole of Arena Primus, which was at the time hosting a grand parade for Slavious Doom in preparation for the overlord's expected acquisition: the legendary Blade of Fire.

CHAPTER VIII

THE END OF PRIMUS

'Up ahead!' Decimus screamed, as he dashed along the sloping tunnel. 'There's a green glowing light up ahead!'

The passageways had collapsed all around them, great rocks sealing off their escape in every direction. They would hurry down one long corridor, only to be cut off at the last moment by a giant rock or a column of collapsing rubble.

They changed course six, seven, eight times as Decimus and Ruma both took turns to lead the party. Now, finally, they had seen a light at the end of the tunnel, a light that was bright, shimmering and entirely natural rather than the glowing emerald flare they had come to expect in this subterranean hell.

Decimus had acquired a second wind; he dashed up the tunnel as if he were running downhill. Ruma and Olu weren't far behind him, and Argon was using every tired muscle in an attempt to propel himself forward. Even Gladius was keeping up.

Half tripping, half tumbling over yet another section of collapsing wall, Decimus scrambled to his feet and took three final leaps forward, running up, up, up . . . and disappearing into the light.

Ruma was next, collapsing on to the hot dirt and coughing in a series of fits and bursts. Olu was the first to emerge from the tunnels on his feet, but

even he staggered slightly when Argon ran
into him. Eventually, puffing, panting and
cursing the gods and the land in general,
Gladius padded out of the groundwork and
dropped to his knees.

'We're free!' Decimus cried, his voice
ringing out like the chime of a great bell. 'We
are FREEEEEE!!!!'

Argon pointed with a trembling finger,
and when he spoke his voice was bursting
with barely concealed excitement.

'The arena!' he shouted. 'Look at the
arena!'

Ruma, Olu and Gladius all turned around,
very slowly, and set their eyes upon the
building they had been forced to call home
for so long.

Arena Primus had collapsed so completely that it was as if a great magician had clicked his fingers and made it vanish. All that was left of the once dominant structure was a series of half-destroyed archways and a lone column that was no bigger than one of the prop towers that had once huddled in the shadows of its outer wall.

'It's gone,' said Olu, in total astonishment. 'It's totally gone. Do you think Doom was inside?'

'We can only hope,' said Ruma, with a tired grin. 'I say "good riddance" to them both.'

'What about us?' Gladius said, still half in a daze from the energy he'd expended during the tunnel dash. 'What are we going to do?'

Decimus Rex walked over to the big slave

and threw a friendly arm over his shoulders.

'We go home,' he said, hugging Gladius

tightly as the other slaves came to stand

around them, all bearing a variety of joyous,

lopsided grins. 'We go home.'

Decimus raised his hands in the air, and let out an incredible cry of victory. The other slaves all roared their approval.

Eventually, after swearing never to let a

year go by without meeting once again, all the slaves went their separate ways. Argon and Ruma went north together, while Decimus, Gladius and Olu headed east. The slaves, who had started out as six, now walked to freedom as five, the strength of their friendship blazing like a furnace in their hearts, blazing like the Blade of Fire itself.

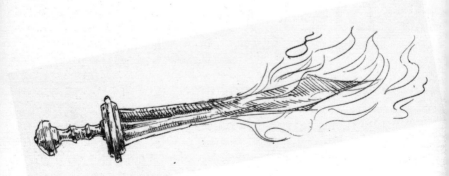

CHAPTER IX

THE SEED OF VENGEANCE

Two days later, deep below the sunken arena in a passage of rough stone somewhere north of the Maw's devastated lair, a section of rubble was moved aside. A large black boot kicked the remaining pebbles from the underground path, and an armoured gauntlet smashed through a jut of crumbling rock that still clung on to the narrow ceiling.

BOOM.

Another distant collapse.

BOOM.

Somewhere ahead and below, a fresh pile of stone fell, sealing the exit of yet another ancient crawl-space.

BOOM.

BOOM.

BOOM.

Slavious Doom stared into the darkness of the tunnel ahead, seeing only more shadows before him. The way back was blocked, the way onward led down . . . down . . . down . . . but to where? To what? Would he escape this hellish maze, or was he doomed to walk the underworld for ever?

Decimus Rex, said a rasping voice in his head. The boy and his cursed friends. They must be made to pay for this. They must be made to suffer.

First, he needed to find a way out of this immense labyrinth. Only then could he find that wretched, hateful, ruinous child. Only then could Slavious Doom take his terrible revenge . . .

COMING IN 2010

A mysterious message brings the surviving slaves of Arena Primus back together, and soon they are locked in a desperate quest to discover the truth behind it. The journey will take Decimus and his friends into the heart of China . . . and, possibly, into the jaws of a deadly trap.

Will Slavious Doom have his dark revenge on the boys, or will they triumph over evil and finally rescue a friend they thought was lost to them . . . for ever.

GLADIATOR BOY

BATTLE IN THE EAST
THE GOLDEN WARRIOR

ARENA COMBAT

Get ready to challenge your friends! Each Gladiator Boy book will contain a different trial – collect them all to run your own Arena of Doom – either at home or in the school playground.

TRIAL 6

THE RACE

In Gladiator Boy: The Blade of Fire, Decimus had to race through a labyrinth in order to find and rescue his friends, and to retrieve the fabled 'Blade of Fire'. In this sixth trial, a race will be held – will you be fast enough?

GAME PROCEDURE

The race must be run on grass and NOT on a hard surface of any kind.

The referee must set a finish line, which must be at least half a football pitch away from the players' starting line.

The referee then stands beside the players and counts down to the start. On your marks, get set, go! The player who wins the race is declared the Grand Gladiator of the trials!

This trial, like the others, is played by taking on the character of a slave from Gladiator Boy. The profile in the following pages will add to your growing collection of characters!

CHARACTER PROFILE
DECIMUS

NAME: Decimus Rex

FROM: Tarentum

HEIGHT: 1.73 metres

BODY TYPE: Muscular, slight

BEST END: Gladius

CELLMATE: Gladius

DECIMUS QUIZ: How well do you know Decimus? Can you answer the following three questions?

1. WHO DOES DECIMUS RESCUE FIRST IN THE LABYRINTH BENEATH ARENA PRIMUS?

2. WHO IS WITH DECIMUS WHEN HE FIRST ENCOUNTERS THE CYCLOPS?

3. WHO DOES DECIMUS SAY CAN FIGHT 'ANYONE'? IS IT ARGON, RUMA OR GLADIUS?

Answers: 1. Olu, book 5 2. Olu and Gladius, page 34 3. Ruma, page 66

WEAPON
PROFILE
THE TRIDENT

The trident is a fork,
or three-pronged spear.

It is often associated with the gods, and was said to be used by the Hindu god Shiva, the Roman god Neptune and the Greek god Poseidon.

The trident was also used by fishermen, to spear fish in the water.

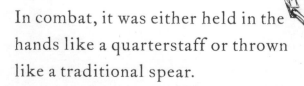

In combat, it was either held in the hands like a quarterstaff or thrown like a traditional spear.

GLADIATOR BOY

Check out the Gladiator Boy website for games, downloads, activities, sneak previews and lots of fun! You can even get extra pieces of the arena and fantastic action figures! Sign up to the newsletter to receive exclusive extra content and the opportunity to enter special competitions.

WWW.GLADIATORBOY.COM

LET BATTLE COMMENCE!

MAKE YOUR OWN ARENA OF DOOM

1. Carefully cut around the outline of the arena section. Ask an adult to help if necessary.
2. Fold across line A. Use a ruler to get a straight edge.
3. Fold across line B. Use a ruler to get a straight edge.
4. Ask an adult to help you score along lines C & D with a pair of sharp scissors.
5. Fold up over line E and push the window out.
6. Repeat instructions 1 to 5 for every Arena of Doom piece collected.
7. Glue the top of each tab and stick them to the next piece of the arena. Repeat as necessary.

CHECK OUT THE WEBSITE FOR A PHOTO OF THE COMPLETE ARENA.

TO MAKE YOUR ACTION FIGURE

1. Cut around the outline of the figure. Ask an adult to help if necessary.
2. Cut along slot X at the bottom of the figure.
3. Cut out Gladiator Boy rectangle.
4. Cut along slot Y.
5. Slot figure into slot Y.